ATHUNIUM

by Umar Arar

Athunium

LULU

Copyright ©2012 by Umar Arar

The moral right of the author has been asserted.

All characters and events in this publication, other than those clearly in the public domain, are fictitious and any resemblance to real persons, living or dead, is purely coincidental.

All Rights Reserved.

No part of this publication may be reproduced, stored in a retrieval system, or transmitted in any form or by any means, without the prior permission in writing of the publisher, nor be otherwise circulated in any form of binding or cover other than that in which it is published and without a similar condition including this condition being imposed on the subsequent purchaser.

ISBN 978-1-4716-8373-2

Printed and bound in Great Britain courtesy of Lulu Enterprises, Inc.

www.lulu.com

Umar Arar

For my princess Laura and my adorable boys Rocky and Zack.

Athunium

Umar Arar

Acknowledgements

*There are so many people that I want to thank, I've had a lot of support from a lot of people.
If I forget you, I am really sorry!!!*

*First of all, my wife and soul mate Laura. She shared this story with me plenty of times over the years, before I put it down on paper. She enjoyed hearing it every time.
I can't do anything without thanking my two boys Rocky and Zack, every ounce of inspiration I have comes from them, and I do everything for them.*

All my Facebook friends who showed me massive support when I announced that this book was coming, Justin, Lori, Dylan, Laura M., Luke, Mat W., Misty, Sarah, Jamie, Rita, Anna, Pernille, Alex, Ian, John, Claudia, Iva, Matilda, Lance, Jan, Angela, Malwi, Basher, Caine, Shreyash, Pauline, Waseem, Shannon, Colin, Wiebke, George, Adrian, Rohan and Martijn. Thank you so much guys!

I also gotta thank my Mum, Dad and all my brothers and sisters, Taha, Saffeyah, Saadi, Aziz, Anees, Hamdi and Mariam! Love you guys!

My bros from 3 Doors Down, Brad, Chris, Todd, Matt, Greg, Judah, Chet, Robbie and Phin, you guys gave me the confidence to do something about all these ideas!

Finally, the guy that put my butt into gear to finally write this book, my bro from Primark, Zak. Thanks man!

Athunium

CONTENTS

Chapter 1: The Discovery……...…………..………8
Chapter 2: Behold Ayva and the
   Galactic Federation of Light………....17
Chapter 3: The Story……………………………...24
Chapter 4: Journey to Vega…………………….31
Chapter 5: Learning the impossible……………......41
Chapter 6: The stolen Beamship…………………...47
Chapter 7: Mission: Protect Earth……………....56
Chapter 8: Return to space,
   Enter Ratiuch!…..…………...………65
Chapter 9: Alpha Draconis……………….…......71
Chapter 10: The Showdown…………………......77

CHAPTER 1
The Discovery

The sun set as usual on the night of Monday 1st January 2001, deep in the suburbs of London after the New Year's celebrations. Where most people were heading off to bed, other's stayed up till dawn to party some more. But for one 19 year old teenager, this one night would change his entire life.

Kyle was one of those average kids, dark wavy hair, brown eyes, not too tall and he was really into his music. His parents, brother and sister all settled down for the night. Kyle sat up in his bed, unable to sleep from all the noise outside.

The hours went by, he was still sitting up.

Although all the partying had stopped, something was still keeping him up. Sitting in the dark, in the quiet, he stared out of his bedroom window, gazing at the stars, he thought to himself *I'd love to see them close up one day...* and slowly he drifted off to sleep.

He dreamt of visiting the stars, he flew through space and passed the planet Mars up close, the stars began to fly past him, he was picking up speed until he flew into a dark cloud, he couldn't see a thing, then a pair of big red eyes with slits for pupils began to come closer and closer and soon he began to hear a distant soft whisper.

"Kyle... Kyle...KYLE!!" Kyle woke up fast in panic; he then turned to his bedroom door to find Adam, his brother, standing there white as a ghost.

"I heard a voice" Adam shuddered, "It was saying my name over and over."

"I heard it too." said Kyle, confused, he began to wonder what was going on.

Then the voice filled their ears again, this time, louder, sounding desperate.

"Come outside, come to me, there is something you've got to know, I need you right away."

Adam and Kyle looked at each other instantly, Kyle looking dumbfounded but Adam afraid, Adam was younger than Kyle by a few years.

Kyle stopped for a second just trying to understand what was happening, he began to get all hot and bothered, "Let's go outside then."

"No way!" howled Adam, "I'm not going out there!"

Kyle got up out from his bed slowly and put on his slippers, he walked towards Adam and looked at him in the eye, "Do you think we're going crazy?" Adam stared back at Kyle, not saying a word, the voice spoke again.

"Come to me, I will guide you."

"C'mon we've gotta go, I need to see what this is!" Kyle attempted to usher Adam down the stairs. "Get your shoes on!"

"I'm not going Kyle, I don't wanna go!" Adam cried "I'm telling Mum and Dad, I'm scared!"

"No!" whispered Kyle "Don't tell Mum and Dad anything, wait until I get back!"

Adam looked at Kyle with tears running down his face and cried again "I'm scared!"

"Shh!" whispered Kyle "Don't say anything OK? OK?!"

"OK." Stopped Adam as Kyle made his way down the stairs towards the front door.

It was still dark outside, as the front door of a house opened; Kyle slowly stepped out. He looked back at the radio clock hanging up on the wall inside, it said "Monday 1st January 2001, 4:32 am." He slowly closed the door behind himself and made his way into the low lit street.

He walked up the road, slowly, waiting for the voice to guide him; he continued to walk around for a few minutes, but to no avail. The voice never spoke.

He turned to walk back home, he walked up to his front door and laughed to himself "I knew I was going crazy." Then he heard the voice again "You're not going crazy, make your way to the open grassland, quickly."

He stopped and thought hard of what the open grassland would have meant and then he remembered him and his girlfriend Emily's favourite hanging spot, the park around the corner.

So, Kyle made his way to the park. It was dark and gloomy, he couldn't see much at all. He swallowed his anxiety and kept on walking into the dark, empty, quiet and vast park. Then through the trees he caught a glimpse of a light, he chose to walk towards it. He knew this area well, *there shouldn't be a light there, there's a wall behind that tree…* He thought to himself.

The closer he got to the light, the brighter it became. Soon enough he was standing at least a meter from the tree that was emanating this now blinding bright light, then all of a sudden a silhouette of a woman appeared through the beams.

Shocked, Kyle looked on into the light, "hello?" he muttered.

Out of the light stepped a beautiful woman, long blonde hair, fair skin, bright blue eyes. She was wearing a skin tight silver coloured outfit that resembled a jumpsuit.

There was strange apparatus attached to her belt and an obscure symbol that looked a little bit like the letter W was printed to left of her chest.

W.

In a soft voice, the same voice that called out to him and Adam, she spoke "Thank you for coming Kyle, where's is your brother?"

Kyle continued to look on in shock, not saying a word. The woman looked at him softly and then broke a smile, "I understand you are uneasy, it's OK, and I am a friend."

She walked towards him and placed her hand on his shoulder, "Kyle, you can trust me" she looked at him in the eye, "come with me" she finished, with a soft smile. She turned her back and walked back into the light.

Kyle began to relax after the physical contact with this strange woman. Although still slightly uneasy, he chose to follow her into the light. He walked forward towards the light between the trees it got so bright that he couldn't see. He continued to keep walking expecting to walk into the wall, but he didn't hit, instead the soft ground changed to hard and the noise of nature was replaced with a quiet humming.

He opened his eyes and was taken by complete surprise. He was no longer in the park, he looked behind himself for reassurance, but there was no way the park could have just disappeared like that.

He looked back around to find himself in a silver metal lined room, a room like he had never seen before, there wasn't even a door. In the middle of the room stood the woman and to her right was what seemed to be a control unit of sorts.

"Welcome to my ship, Kyle." She said with a smile. "For starters, I'm not from your planet, the one that you call Earth. I am a Pleiedian, my name is Simien."

Kyle looked at her and slowly began to smile "Now this is an awesome dream."

"This is no dream Kyle." Simien said with a serious look. "This is reality. I have come to you because you and your brother are descendants from an ancient race called the Xornans, there is an issue in the Hetra galaxy and your help is needed Kyle."

"The what?" Kyle laughed.

"The Athunium is in danger, if we don't stop it the whole universe will implode and everything as you know it will cease to exist..."

"Hold on just a minute." Kyle stopped Simien midsentence "You're expecting me to believe that I'm an alien, you're an alien and everything that you've just told me about this aluminium, or whatever you call it, is all true?"

"It's Athunium." She stated "and yes I am expecting you to believe it, you have to believe it."

Kyle rudely grinned "Yeah, OK, whatever."

"Look through the viewing panel." Simien ordered, pointing towards a window in the room.

Kyle walked over to the window and looked through it, his facial expression changed; his eyes grew wide as he found himself looking upon Planet Earth itself.

"H…how did you do that?" asked Kyle.

"My Beamship" said Simien "With this ship, I can travel freely through time and space."

"I… I don't believe you." Said Kyle "Cool trick 'n all, but we we're just in the park, I was just in the park. I don't even…"

"I will prove it to you." Simien interrupted. "What do you want to see?"

Kyle turned and looked at Simien, he cracked a grin.

"Show me… the stars."

CHAPTER 2
Behold Ayva and the Galactic Federation of Light

Simien walked towards her control unit and pushed some buttons, the ship suddenly filled with a big *whoosh*, Kyle watched out the window, the view of Earth distorted quickly then a spiralling vortex engulfed the ship, within seconds it was all over. He was looking over a new solar system, more beautiful than his own.

A bright sun shone in the distance. Orbiting it were six planets, all with their own moons. This was unlike anything the people of Earth had ever seen, bright shades of purple, blue, orange and even yellow.

The planets were all shimmering like marbles in the sunlight.

"Welcome to *my* home." Smiled Simien, "This, is the Pleiades system. My planet, Ayva is the purple one."

Kyle's eyes glistened, he couldn't comprehend the stunning beauty that this solar system beheld, he was speechless he couldn't even move.

"Would you like visit my planet?" she asked.

"Please…" it was the only word he was able to get out.

Ayva began to come closer, growing rapidly in size, or so it seemed.

He came to realise that it was the Beamship moving towards the planet at high speed. Soon the ship pierced the atmosphere and descended rapidly towards the ground, then touched down slowly.

Simien walked towards the wall of the ship, "Are you coming?" she asked a very bewildered Kyle.

"There's... no door. How do we get out?" he asked.

"We got in, didn't we?" she smiled again, reaching for the wall in front of her, as soon as her fingertip touched the metal, the wall rippled like water, then as if it had turned to liquid the metal spiralled apart revealing an opening to the outside.

Simien stepped out, Kyle followed. To his surprise he stepped out onto blue grass, he looked up at the sky it was aglow with a hint of purple, he saw two other huge planets lay in the distance, it was night time and bugs that seemed like fireflies lit up the air.

"The colours... the planets…" he muttered "is it *even* possible?"

"The universe is full of miraculous secrets Kyle, not all things are as beautiful and heavenly as what you see."

Kyle looked at her and smiled "I think… I believe you now." He nodded as he spoke.

"Are you hungry?" she asked walking towards a tree, it had natural brown coloured bark, but blue leaves and hanging from the tree were an odd shaped, orange coloured fruit.

"Yeah, I'm starving!" he chuckled "It feels like I haven't eaten for like a whole day!"

"You haven't." she added picking a fruit from the tree, "We call this Vermina, in my opinion, the tastiest thing you will ever eat."

Not thinking about what Simien had just said, he snatched the fruit from her hand and sunk his teeth into it, orange coloured juices ran from his mouth and where he bit into it, his eyes closed in pleasure, he finished the Vermina in just under a few big bites.

"That was amazing!" he shouted, licking the juices from his fingers and lips, he ran to the tree to grab another.

"Kyle, one is enough." Kyle stopped and turned to her "your stomach is not used to that sort of food yet, if you eat any more than that, you may get ill. Besides, eating just one Vermina will cure your hunger and thirst for an entire week."

"OK." said Kyle, looking slightly disappointed.

"Now onto more important matters, let's get you some proper clothes."

Later, Kyle walked out from the Beamship dressed in a black coloured robe, similar to a martial artist gi and obi. A yellow line flowed across each hem. The same symbol on Simien's clothing also adorned Kyle's in silver.

"You are now dressed properly for the council. Follow me." She said.

"The council?" Kyle asked, confused.

Simien took Kyle and they walked through a stone pathway which led to what seemed to be a glass dome structure, each pane of glass held its own obscure symbol, obviously they were letters from an alien language.

ⵍⵀⵙⵜ ⴼⵛⵀⵓⵢ ⵇ ⵍⵀⴷⵉⴼ

"What does that say?" he asked.

"You'll find out now" she answered, taking him inside. They both walked through into an open hall, "You'll now see so many types of people, from all different races, from so many different galaxies all over the universe."

"*Aliens?*" he questioned.

"You could say that." She finished.

Suddenly a bellowing male voice filled the room "Silence!"

Kyle and Simien stood still in a circle in the middle of the room surrounded by tall wooden lecterns and sitting behind them were hundreds of aliens, all of them with a different appearance; it was almost as if it was a big courthouse.

There was one old man, who looked like he was from Earth, stood up in the centre of the lectern in front of them. "Simien!" he bellowed, "The Galactic Federation of Light has assigned you a mission! What in the creators name are you doing back here?! And, with this… child?!"

"Father…" Simien spoke and she knelt down on one knee, Kyle copied her, though not quite understanding what was going on.

"This boy, he is one of the last of the Xornans, legend for tells of the last, with the power to save the universe from the Rep..."

"I know what the legend states!" the man interrupted, this man was the father of Simien, his name was Ardóne "And you are sure he is the one?"

"I am sure father, more sure than I have ever been of anything." Simien looked straight at her father with determination in her eyes.

"Then we must brief and train this young boy, we are running out of time."

"Lord Ardóne! How can you trust her word?" A blue skinned man with a long white beard stood up and challenged Kyle's authenticity.

"Relax Izukaur, I can trust my daughter's word. I now feel the Xornan spirit emanating from his aura. Simien, take the boy to Vega. Train him for three years in the ancient art of Xornan mythology. If he is the one the legends speak of, that should be more than enough time for his true power to shine through. Explain the situation to him on the way. Go! Now!"

"Yes father."

CHAPTER 3
The Story

The Beamship rose from the Ayvan soil then darted up and out of the atmosphere, meanwhile inside.

"Can you just tell me what the hell is going on?" Kyle said.

"I am not forcing you to help Kyle, but I must tell you about what is happening either way. Over 100 million years ago, the planet you live on now was inhabited by a race of people called the Reptilians. They dominated the planet for thousands of years and lived alongside what you know as the Dinosaurs. But since the giant asteroid hit the Earth 65 million years ago, the Reptilians fled with our help.

Since then the planet had re-stabilised and people from all over the stars began to inhabit this world that was only inhabited by sea creatures and land organisms. We decided to help these newly found civilisations with technology and helped them to build complex structures that would last for years, which are quite a lot of the large structures you see today."

"Like the pyramids?" Kyle asked.

"Yes, we helped with those. They would have had no other way of carrying stones weighing one to two tonnes on their own.

Anyway, as I was saying, the humans as you know them evolved into their own cultures and communities, I am really proud to have been a part in helping build that.

But now, the Reptilians want their home back. They're also angry at us for aiding the new civilisations growth. The king, only known as Blackmist, has declared war on us and plans to use Athunium, which is the universal energy, to power a space armada and drag their new planet Alpha Draconis through space, to Earth where they will invade and re-populate Earth as a Reptilian planet.

The Athunium would not be able to take that sort of strain, Alpha Draconis is a giant planet, and so is their armada, all that energy would cause the Athunium to implode, ripping our galaxy to shreds.

That's where you come in, legend for tells of a descendant of the Xornan race will rise up and thwart the Reptilian rebellion and save the universe from imminent danger."

"Wow… that's a lot to take in, man." Kyle muttered.

"I'll take you back home and give you twenty-four hours to think about it. When you're ready, just think of me and I will be here, I will be able to telepathically hear you." Simien explained.

"OK Simien, thank you." Kyle smiled at her, he walked towards the wall and pressed it with his finger, the wall rippled and then opened just like before, Kyle looked out into the park that they first left from, he stepped out.

"See you soon." She said and the Beamship lit up and darted up at incredible speed into the night sky.

Kyle watched it go till it faded like a star in the distance. He made his way home, and was unbelievably tired. He opened his front door and looked at the digital clock.

"What? Monday 1ˢᵗ January 2001, 4:33 am?! How could I have been only gone a minute?!"

Adam came down the stairs, still scared "What's wrong…? Why haven't you gone yet?"

Kyle thought about what had just happened, and then he remembered something that Simien said *"With this ship, I can travel freely through **time** and **space**."*

Then Kyle said, "Don't worry little bro, you wouldn't believe me even if I told you, c'mon lets go to bed, I'm tired!"

Sunrise shone through Kyle's bedroom window; the light hit his face and woke him up. He turned around to find Emily, his girlfriend, sitting on the edge of his bed. "You're Mum and Dad let me in, are you ok? You've been sweating in your sleep."

"Yeah…" groaned Kyle, "I'm OK." He said as he sat up, "Just had a weird dream, that's all."

"Well I've got something to show you." Smiled Emily getting a little excited, she pulled out a white stick from her jacket pocket.

"Is that a…?"

"Pregnancy test! Yes it is!" interrupted Emily with a huge smile on her face. "I'm pregnant Kyle! We're gonna have a baby!"

"Whoa, hold on, hold on." Kyle pushed the pregnancy test away from him "This is a lot to take in, babe, I've had a lot to take in today."

"I know, but isn't it just great!" she hugged him and kissed him "I'll see you later OK?" she got up and went to walk out and noticed the black coloured robes from Simien folded up on his computer chair. "Hold on, where did you get that from? I've never seen it before…"

Kyle saw it and then it hit him that it was all real, he swung himself out of bed and said "Ahh, that! Errm… it was a New Year's present, from… a friend!"

"OK…" Emily eyed at Kyle with a slight hint of suspiciousness. "I'll see you later anyway, I love you." And she walked out.

"I love you too." Kyle replied.

Kyle sat on the edge of his bed, thinking about what to do. He could be the one to save the entire universe and could be a father; he kept on going over that again and again in his head.

Soon he grew to realise that this child would give him the motivation to fight, the child would give him something to fight for. He was ready.

He got dressed into the black Pleiedian robes. He then closed his eyes and thought hard "Simien, I am ready."

A blinding flash of light engulfed him, and he found himself standing among Simien and two other men in Simien's Beamship.

"Kyle, I am so glad that you have decided to aid us in the battle. I would like you to meet my brothers, Joakum and Ingris."

They both looked and dressed similar to Simien, only having shorter hair and more manly features.

"They will aid me in your training. We only have three years to unleash your inner power!"

"Not really" Kyle interrupted, "with you, I've got all the time in the world, you can travel through time remember!"

"Negative bro." interrupted Ingris "A lot of events are stuck at a fixed points in time, your power gain and the battle, it's all time locked. It's a legend waiting to happen. We cannot mess with that, we can only guide you. That is the Ayvan nature."

"So we have no time to lose." Said Simien, "then let's go!"

CHAPTER 4
Journey to Vega

"We will start your training here in the Beamship, we need to make sure that you will be used to the gravity on Vega. Simien had gravity enhancements installed in the ship today just for your training" Ingris exclaimed. "If you we're a normal human your bones would not be strong enough to take double of your native gravity. But you're not. You have Xornan bones inside you, the strongest race in the universe. Are you ready Kyle?"

Kyle looked at Ingris with confidence. "I'm ready."

"OK." Joakum said, pressing a button on the control unit. "Initiate gravity enhancement five times that of Earth!"

Suddenly Kyle hit the floor, with a tremendous crash! "Argh! I'm… too… heavy…!"

Kyle struggled to even breathe. It felt as though his body weight tripled in seconds.

"This is how your training starts Kyle." Ingris exclaimed. "You must be able to hold yourself up effortlessly in this gravity before we can move on! Is that understood?"

"Under… stood" Kyle struggled to get the words out, trying to force himself up off the floor, sweat began to drip from his nose. It was taking every bit off effort in his body to at least hold his head up.

Joakum gave Kyle some advice. "Close your eyes and empty your mind. You are not as heavy as you feel."

The hours passed and Kyle was still struggling to hold his head up.

Simien watched on and added "You *can* do it, Kyle. Just remember who you are doing it for."

Simien's words echoed inside his head, all he kept thinking about was Emily and the child and what would happen when the ruthless Blackmist got to Earth. The intensity of thought grew and grew then with a piercing cry he lifted himself off from the floor and held himself up on his feet.

"I… did it!" He panted, and broke a smile.

The other three smiled back at him, "I'm proud of you Kyle" said Simien.

Then Kyle came over all weak and collapsed onto the floor, he blacked out.

Later, Kyle opened his eyes to see Simien nursing him. "How're you feeling?" she asked.

"Tired…" laughed Kyle, "I can't believe I actually did it…"

Simien put her hand across his forehead, "There is still so much more to learn when you recover, when you are ready Ingris and Joakum with teach you the ancient art of Xornan close combat. Get some more rest."

Kyle sat up, "No, I've gotta do it now! I need to make sure I am as strong as possible for Blackmist!"

"That's what I like to hear!" Ingris stood by Simien, with a smile, "You're already strong kid. Not even I did as well as that on my first time on the gravity test! It's not easy!"

"Thanks man." Said Kyle gratefully, "I've gotta keep Emily safe. She's pregnant with my child."

"Then lets hurry up and do this, you have something to fight for kid, I treasure that in a person."

Kyle followed Ingris onto the main deck of the ship.

"Are you ready for the gravity enhancement again?"

"I was born ready." Kyle smiled with confidence.

Joakum stood by the control desk again, pressed a button and said "Initiate gravity enhancement five times that of Earth!"

"Brace yourself!" added Ingris.

The gravity instantly changed, Kyle almost lost his balance but he kept himself upright.

"Well done, now it's time to teach you the ancient art of Xornan close combat!" shouted Ingris "First watch me and Joakum, we will perform an example!"

"OK" said Kyle.

He watched as Joakum and Ingris, fought in a magical way, darting around the place landing heavy blows against each other, this was an ancient martial arts fighting style from a different planet, it was almost like a dance.

After an hour or so of close combat, they both stopped by somersaulting into a kneeling position.

"That was amazing!" said Kyle in amazement. "I gotta learn how to do that!"

"You will already know once you start" said Ingris, he got up and walked toward Kyle, "It's in your blood."

Ingris braced himself and moved into a strange fighting stance, he was crouched with his legs apart; his right arm was in front for defence and the other arm behind him, ready for attack.

Kyle faced Ingris and copied the exact stance he held.

"This is the most important stance you will ever need to know, it's holds maximum attack power and maximum defence power! You now need to know about dealing blows to your enemy, it's important that you get this right Kyle. If you slip up, it could leave you open to a deadly attack and Reptilians are ruthless!"

Ingris then began to teach Kyle about the correct way to punch and kick his opponents while keeping his defences intact. The teaching session went on what seemed like for weeks.

Kyle's fighting style was growing and fast. Every week Simien brought in a Vermina for everyone to eat. This was great as it meant for less time eating and more time training without getting hungry or thirsty.

It had now been just over a year and Kyle looked much older and much stronger, he could now hold his own in a two-on-one fight against both Ingris and Joakum.

Later that afternoon, they were all sitting around a fire back on Ayva; they were watching the reflections of the other planets in the water when Simien said "I think you are now ready for the next step Kyle."

"What is it?" Kyle replied.

"You've now got to learn how to control Athunium" added Joakum.

"What do you mean control it?"

"Remember when I said to you before about Athunium being universal energy?" Simien asked.

"Yeah, I remember that."

"Well we are all able to control it and use it to our advantage, which is what Blackmist is doing to move Alpha Draconis."

"We're going to teach you how can use it for an offensive purpose, you'd be able to control the energy with your own will, like this…" Ingris opened his hand up towards the fire and blue wisps of energy slowly shot from his palm and doused the fire.

"That was so cool!" Kyle said in amazement, "There are so many crazy things out here! Man, who knows what's next!"

"Kyle, you must focus" stressed Simien, "We must soon make our way to Vega where we will teach you how to control Athunium and we can then we can try and take on Blackmist."

"Well then let's go!" Kyle stood up, raring to go. "We have one year and eight months till the time is up, we might as well get going!"

Simien smiled "you are never patient, are you?" She stood up, and the others followed, they walked toward the Beamship, suddenly a red ball of energy shot out from the doorway and slammed Joakum to the ground.

"Joakum!" screamed Simien, running to her brother's aid.

"What was that?!" screamed Kyle.

"A Reppie scout!" answered Ingris angrily "Let's get him Kyle!"

Kyle and Ingris charged toward the Beamship, another energy ball shot out, this time heading for Ingris, it narrowly missed. The Reptilian jumped out from the Beamship heading straight for Kyle.

Kyle froze in horror, it was like a human, but it had green scaly skin, a lizard shaped head and yellow eyes with slits for the pupils. It was screaming an ear piercing hiss. Flying towards him, it opened its claws for an attack.

Then, SLAM! A blue beam of energy hit it hard from the side and slammed it lifelessly to the ground.

It was all over in a couple of seconds. Kyle turned to see Ingris with his hands smoking from beam he had just made.

"I wouldn't exactly call that a good start" snapped Ingris.

"I… I'm sorry…" muttered Kyle.

"What were you thinking?! Standing there like that, you've could've been killed!"

"Ingris!" Simien called, "Joakum's in pretty bad shape…"

Ingris ran to Simien who was cradling a burnt Joakum in her arms, Kyle walked over, "Is he gonna be OK?"

"I don't know…" Simien said, as a tear ran down her face "I don't think he's going to make it…"

Kyle began to apologise "I'm sorry… I…"

"Don't be sorry, Kyle" Simien stood up and put her hand on his shoulder, "you didn't know what to expect from a Reptilian when you first saw one, I understand. They're horrifying beasts."

"Then you all better go… to Draconia Minor first. Get this kid used to seeing those things…" coughed Joakum. "Take him Ingris, and teach him. Otherwise…" he coughed again, "plenty more innocent… people will meet my fate…"

Ingris knelt down by his brother's side, holding his hand. "I'm here brother."

Joakum's grip on Ingris' hand fell loose "good…bye…brother…" he began to fade and then he slowly passed away, his body began to turn into energy.

The energy floated up to the floor, it was like smoke, but floated slowly and more soothingly the energy then floated towards Kyle. It surrounded him for a few seconds then joined with his body.

For a few minutes Kyle entire body glowed in a beautiful hue of blue energy.

"He's a part of you now, Kyle" Simien sniffed, wiping away the tears in her eyes.

"How do you feel?" Ingris asked.

Kyle looked at Simien and said "I feel good. It's like I can actually feel the energy flowing through my body"

Simien swallowed her hurt and then said "Now we must teach you how to expel it, let us take a trip to Vega, and then we will go to Draconia Minor, just like Joakum said, so you can hone your skills before the battle."

CHAPTER 5
Learning the impossible

Deep in the far reaches of the Hetra Galaxy, a large murky green planet span around a single red dwarf star, above it stood an enormous dark grey warship double the size of the planet itself.

In the primary control deck, looking out the viewing screen stood a tall dark purple coloured Reptilian, with a long tail, he wore a long red cape attached over black coloured chest armour with an insignia on the right side of the chest.

His mouth began to move, he hissed and with his deep gurgling voice he spoke. "Soon, our home will be mine to rule once again. The day those Pleiedians chose to betray us over our home will be regretted."

A shorter green Reptilian commando walked into the room followed by another five. It then spoke "My Lord Blackmist. Permission to speak?"

"Granted" said Blackmist, still looking outside over the planet.

"We sent a scout after the girl as you requested, but it seems that some problems have arisen."

"What problems?" grunted Blackmist fiercely.

"The scout was killed sire, blasted down by her brother."

"Never mind, send another!"

"But sire they have attained a Xornan as an ally."

"Hmm… that could be a problem" Blackmist turned around and looked at the Reptilian commando. "Find the Xornan and bring him to me alive."

"Affirmative my lord" replied the commando who then left the room with the others.

Blackmist turned back to the viewing panel and said "It looks like I may have to start my plans early. No matter…" he began to laugh uncontrollably getting louder and louder.

Back in the Pleiades System Simien's Beamship left Ayva and headed two planets up in orbit, Vega.

The ship lowered down into the atmosphere of the muddy yellow planet.

The ship lowered down through what seemed to be a heavy sandstorm, it then touched down in what appeared to be a vast desert.

Simien, Ingris and Kyle stepped out of the ship and were buffeted by the sandstorms.

The raging winds were almost deafening.

Simien shouted through the noise "This is where we train your ability to control the Athunium by your own will!"

Kyle shouted back "OK! What have I got to do?"

Then suddenly the noise stopped and the sandstorm was no longer buffeting them, he turned to see Ingris focusing with his eyes closed, he was holding a shield over the three of them blocking out anything from getting in.

"That is the first thing you have to try" exclaimed Simien "using your mind and energy to create a shield, it's the most basic form of use."

"OK, how do I do it?"

"It's all about focus. You must open your mind to everything around you."

So Kyle closed his eyes and completely relaxed.

"Next, you must feel it inside you. You must be at one with the energy around you. You must visualise it in everything you see, and then control it with your imagination."

Kyle visualised that blue wispy energy that he saw back on Ayva. In his head he saw it all around him. He imagined hard that it surrounded the three of them creating a shield. "OK, I think I got it."

"Then I will release my shield!" said Ingris, as he said that he let his shield down then all of a sudden the sandstorm crashed back into them knocking them all into the desert ground.

They all howled in pain as the raging sandstorm buffeted them even harder than before.

Kyle forced himself up the deafening wind was smacking him from all directions. He closed his eyes and tried again but the more he tried the harder the wind fought back. "Why does it fight back every time I try?!" he shouted.

"That's why my father chose Vega for your training!" Ingris replied "This planet's atmosphere tests your strengths to the limit. He wanted to make sure you had the maximum training plane, your power needs to have tripled by the time the battle comes!"

*I must do this. I have to do this. I **can** do this.* Kyle kept repeating those words in his head, the more he tried to control the energy, the more it fought back.

The desert was desolate, the raging storms were restless. The minutes turned to hours, the hours turned into days and the days turned into weeks and the weeks turned into months. It was trying to make the impossible possible.

Nothing was working. The more he tried, the more the storms fought back. Simien and Ingris' patience was unbelievable.

How did Ingris do it? And so instantly… maybe a human can't do it? Maybe a human wasn't meant to do it?

Kyle began to question himself, this was impossible. He couldn't do it. No matter how hard he focused, no matter how hard he pushed he couldn't control the Athunium to even shield himself from wind. How could he use it in an offensive way, just like that Reptilian did, just like Ingris did, he also began to get frustrated with himself.

Suddenly a strange voice spoke through the storm "you doubt yourself too much boy!"

The three of them turned to see a silhouette standing near them through the raging sand.

"The name's Zarckro."

CHAPTER 6
The stolen Beamship

The sun rose up back on Planet Ayva and the Galactic Federation of Light had organised to hold an important meeting on the Reptilian agenda.

The courtroom had completely changed its appearance from before. Instead, lines of chairs filled the room with only one desk in the middle, as if it was prepared for a lecture. The doors swung open and dressed in a long white robe Lord Ardóne, walked through and stood up at the desk. Although the room and chairs were empty he said "Thank you all for coming."

Suddenly blue beams of light shot down into each of the chairs which were then replaced with all the aliens from the courtroom before.

"I have gathered you all today because we have received word from one of our sources that Blackmist's agenda has been brought forward due to unforeseen circumstances. He has discovered our association with the Xornan boy."

With a flash of white light, a Beamship suddenly crashed through the courtroom wall, wounding a number of federation members.

It looked exactly the same as Simien's; it was silver in colour and was disk shaped. A small dome was situated at the top.

"What is the meaning of this?!" howled Ardóne "A Beamship?!" the ship caused the air in the room to stir, heavy wind whirled around all the people Ardóne looked on in horror as destruction tormented the room and in one more sudden flash of light the ship crashed through the ceiling and left Ayva in seconds.

Smoke swirled around the room revealing a myriad amount of dead bodies, fire and falling ash cloaked the room in a glowing blaze and under a pile of rubble laid an arm adorning a white sleeve.

Meanwhile back on Vega, Kyle was continuing his training, he was screaming and bursting from him was massive amounts of energy pushing back the sandstorm and winds, this time it was him causing the storm, the amount of energy his body was exerting was remarkable.

Ingris and Simien looked on in awe, next to them stood an Insectoid man, he almost looked like half man, half mantis, and he was slouched over.

Then without warning, a box on Simien's belt began to flash red and it began to shriek a deafening alarm. "Something's wrong!" yelled Simien "We must return back home at once!"

The four of them ran towards the Beamship hastily, the boarded the ship and within seconds it darted out of Vega's atmosphere and touched down in Ayva. Simien left the ship first and hurriedly made her way to the Galactic Federation of Light.

But did not expect what she came across next, the entire chambers were in ruins, she then yelled in horror and fell to her knees "NO!"

Ingris ran through into the burning ruins "Father!"

Kyle and Zarckro followed.

Inside, the fires continued to burn and the smoke choked Kyle, Ingris and Zarckro, they were hunting for survivors.

"One of your ships has been stolen, Ingris!" Zarckro claimed.

"How do you know?" Kyle replied.

"He's an Insectoid, Kyle" Ingris added "He's able to look into the recent past see what has just happened. It's a trait that is theirs and only theirs, a reaction from their huge sun back in Zeta Reticuli."

The swirling smoke and ash made it hard to find any survivors.

They all searching through the rubble until Kyle spotted a hand coming out from a pile in the distance, he ran towards it and lifted of big chunks of stone and threw them aside revealing a face that he recognised from before, "Ingris! You're Dad!

Ingris ran to Kyle and knelt down beside him at the lifeless body of his father. "Who did this?!" Ingris screeched in anger and despair clutching Ardóne's body close to his own. He yelled again, "WHO DID THIS?!!"

Simien was still outside and she heard the thoughts of the three inside she began to scream in agony for her father. It was a traumatic moment.

Later outside, Simien was cuddled into her brother whilst Kyle and Zarckro stood outside the ruins, rain began to fall heavily dowsing what was left of the burning rubble.

"No doubt about it." Zarckro abruptly spoke "This was the work of a Reptilian. I sense that there was more than one. And judging from the energy trail that ship left behind, they are heading towards… Earth…"

"What?!" Kyle shouted in horror. He ran towards Simien's ship "C'mon! We've gotta go to Earth! I'm not gonna let them hurt Emily!"

Simien darted up "I agree I will not let those beasts cause anymore grievance in this world!"

Ingris joined them, Zarckro didn't. Insectoids don't go to earth. The federation does not allow it.

The Beamship rushed through a spinning vortex and within seconds, Mother Earth came into view.

"It's good to be home" Kylc smiled at the sight of the planet "but we've got work to do!"

"We've got a signal from the other ship!" Simien found the location of the second ship on her control panel. It was in London! Within seconds the Beamship darted to the surface landing directly next to an identical ship, the door on the other ship was still open.

"They've only just got here, they can't be far." Ingris grunted.

Kyle had realised that they were in the park that he'd first met Simien but he looked around and spotted five Reptilian commandos by the opening and he shouted and ran at them "Hey! Lizard brains!"

Ingris and Simien followed suit, Simien took out a laser gun from her belt and aimed it at the group of Reptilians.

The commandos turned at the three of them and attacked.

A raging fight had broken lose. Kyle and Ingris fought side by side in the Xornan style, dealing heavy blows to these awful creatures, who were also dealing blows back. Simien shot down one leaving herself open to an attack.

Out of the blue in her line of sight rushed a red ball of energy straight for her, she froze. Then it burnt up centimetres from her face, she turned to find Kyle holding up an energy field which blocked the Reptilians deadly blast.

"Thank you Kyle" she smiled.

Kyle turned to find the last Reptilian heading straight for him, he also charged back at it. He jumped up and landed a kick straight to its throat, cutting off it's much needed air supply.

The last Reptilian thumped into the lush green grass, holding its throat, gasping for air.

Ingris walked and looked down upon the beast that was writhing in pain. "That was for what you did to my father" He raised his foot and stamped upon the skull of the creature, blood threw up into the air as its head was crushed into the soil. The five Reptilians lay lifeless in the grass, dead.

"Well done, both of you." Simien said.

Ingris interrupted "No, well done to Kyle! Did you see how he held himself there! That was his first proper fight and he pulled it off with aplomb!"

"I've gotta go see Emily!" Kyle shrieked, "I hope I haven't been away so long that she's already had the baby!"

As he said that, he ran up the road and passed his own home, he missed his old street, he hadn't seen it for a while. Then he stopped a few doors up, he walked across the road and arrived at Emily's house. He knocked on the door.

Emily's mother opened the door. "Oh, it's *you*. What do you want?"

"I need Emily, is she home?" he replied.

"Yeah she's home, with *your* precious family." She replied, slamming the door in his face.

Kyle didn't understand what the hell was going on, so he headed back to his own home and knocked on the door. Simien and Ingris watched from a distance as the door opened.

Kyle's mum was at the door. "Mum!" he said "I'm so happy to see you!"

"Where have you been!" she replied "We've been waiting for you for hours, you should have been back from work ages ago, and what are you wearing!"

Kyle walked in after her to find Emily asleep on the sofa.

He looked up at the radio clock to see that it said "Wednesday 10th January 2001, 8:42pm" *That doesn't even make sense* he thought.

Simien spoke to him telepathically. "Kyle, stay here for a while and look after your family. Those Reptilians most likely won't be the last to come here. You need to protect the planet. I and Ingris on the other hand will leave and we will gather an army for the battle, we will come back for you when you are needed."

Kyle nodded and with that, the contact broke.

CHAPTER 7
Mission: Protect Earth

It was hard getting used to way of life on Earth again… he hadn't slept for almost 2 years. At least now, he got to take a well-deserved rest from all the vigorous training on back on Vega.

That morning, Emily came down the stairs as Kyle was sitting on the sofa in the living room. "It's so nice that your parents have bought me in."

"Yeah" he nodded with a smile.

"I'm the only one who's actually noticed that you've been gone a little over a week, what's going on?"

"Trust me; you wouldn't believe a *word* of it."

"Try me. Not much can surprise me these days." She looked at him hard in the eye. You couldn't get a more serious look out of someone.

Kyle laughed "No need to be so serious!"

"Then tell me where you've been!" she scolded.

"I... I can't..." Kyle sunk back into the sofa. He couldn't look her in the eye.

"Have you been with another girl?" her voice went quiet.

Kyle looked at her, his eyes looked into hers. "...Kind of."

She darted back and yelled at him "Kind of?! What's that supposed to mean?!"

He stood up and shouted back "I told you! You wouldn't believe a word!!" with that, he charged out of the house and slammed the front door behind him.

He walked up the street. Wondering, worried and speculating about how he could explain this whole situation to Emily. These days, if you mentioned aliens and spaceships it means you're crazy.

It's all a world of Science Fiction and fantasy. But in reality it was all more real than anyone ever knew.

Emily followed him out of the house; she ran after him, she wasn't going to let this go. She wanted to find out who he has been with all this time. "I'm pregnant remember! I can't believe that you would abandon me now! Especially when I need you the most! I thought you were better than that Kyle! I thought you were a good person!"

Kyle spun around and stared at Emily with fire in his eyes "Don't you get it?! I am protecting you! That's where I've been this whole time! You and the baby are the most important things in my entire life! I'm doing this for the both of you!"

She screamed back at him "Then explain how that has anything to do with spending over a week with another girl?!"

"It's not like that Emily!" his eyes then grew wide with surprise looking behind Emily. He began to take the Xornan fighting stance "Get down!" he howled.

Emily, curious, turned behind her to see what it was and to her horror stood a six foot tall half man half lizard scowling at her ready to pounce! She shrieked in horror as the monster darted at her with terrifying speeds crying an ear piercing hiss.

From behind her, Kyle dashed to her aid "Arrrgggghhh!!" He slammed his fist into the creatures face with a mighty slam, so hard that it crashed to the floor with a big thud and she fell down from the force of the impact.

Holding its face, the beast growled at Kyle as he looked down on it in confidence.

"You dare attack me!!" it gurgled.

"You dare attack my pregnant girlfriend!!" Kyle replied, kicking the monster in the face breaking its neck, killing it.

Emily lay on the ground and watched in disbelief. Kyle had just protected her from a terrifying monster, Kyle was so strong. She was speechless.

"That's exactly what I was protecting you from." Kyle said calmly. "That was a Reptilian. It's an alien. His race has a plot to take over Earth."

"How… do you know that…?" she replied, shaken.

"That's what I couldn't tell you before, but now you've seen it for yourself, you might as well know…"

Kyle put out his hand and helped her back onto her feet.

"I've been training out in space for almost two years now."

"I thought you looked a little older!" she interrupted looking baffled.

"Yeah… that's the thing. The woman I've been with has been helping train me to fight off those monsters. She is able to travel through time and space in her spaceship. So whenever I leave, I've been brought back almost at the same point as when I left."

"That's incredible…" she said in awe.

"Only problem is…" he continued "is that there are more of those things on the way and they mean war. They're deadly and when I mean more, I'm sure that there are thousands, if not millions!"

"Why are they doing this?" she asked.

"It's a long story. But in a nutshell, Earth used to be their home and they're coming back for it."

"But it's *our* home!" she stated.

"Yeah it is now. The woman I've been with, Simien, told me that I am a descent of a powerful alien race called the Xornans. There is a legend out there, which tells that the last Xornan will save the universe from a deadly threat and Simien's people believe that this is the time the legends talk about and I'm the one spoken of in the legend."

"So you're gonna save the world?" she smiled.

"Yeah I suppose… we'll see." He smiled back.

"Will I get to meet her?"

"I dunno, probably. I mean, she'll come back for me when she has gathered an army to fight. I guess that there's probably going to be more for me to take on that we think!"

"So… you're risking your life to protect me and our child?" she grabbed hold of his arm and pulled him towards her.

"Of course" He gazed into her eyes and pulled her into him and held her close. "You both mean the world to me and I'll do anything in my power to keep you safe."

She gazed back into his eyes and a tear ran down her cheek.

He wiped the tear away, "C'mon, let's go home."

Hand in hand they both walked back to the house.

As the months flew by Emily's pregnancy began to advance. Her abdomen grew gradually. They both went together for tests and scans; they saw the foetus grow into a tiny baby. You would never see a couple so happy and proud.

Then in a sudden turn of events, Emily fell ill just one month from the date the baby was due and was hospitalised. For the nights that followed, Kyle slept on the cold hard hospital floor, always sleeping with one eye open just in case a Reptilian beast tried to pull a fast one.

Emily had been in hospital for almost a week, that morning the doctors came around and said that they had to get the baby out that morning.

So with a sense of urgency Emily was prepped for the operating room. There was no time to induce the birth; she was getting more and more unwell by the day. Kyle was allowed into the operating room to witness the birth of his child.

Later in the operating room the surgeon began the operation with help from other doctors and nurses. Kyle watched as Emily was cut open and within minutes a baby boy emerged, the cord was cut and the baby wrapped in a towel. After a few tests the baby boy was handed to Kyle. "Congratulations!" the nurse cried "You have a beautiful baby boy!"

Kyle looked down on the baby and began to cry, that tiny face, those little fingers all curled up. "My son..." He smiled, still choked up, the tears ran down his face one tear dripped from his nose and landed on the baby's head, the baby squirmed and began to cry.

Weak, Emily watched and smiled "let me see him." She asked.

He turned the baby and showed her, "awww he's gorgeous" she smiled "just like you!"

Kyle smiled back until he heard a voice in his head. "Kyle, it's time."

"Oh no..." Kyle's face went serious. "It's time."

Emily smiled at him "then go save the world, my hero."

CHAPTER 8
Return to space, Enter Ratiuch!

The operating room's doors burst open and Kyle charged out, he ran up the stairs and made his way out of the hospital. As he was running he was ripped off the blue overalls he wore during the operation.

He ran down the steps outside and shouted "Simien! Where are you?!" and in a sudden flash he found himself in a Beamship, but this one was much bigger than the one before. It was almost as if the Beamship had quadrupled in size, there were tens of thousands of different groups of alien races a lot of them were holding onto what looked like futuristic laser guns. Some looked just like earth humans but instead they had blue coloured skin, these were called Sirians from the planet Sirius. Yellow skinned people from Lyra and orange skinned people from Andromeda.

In front of this army stood four people looking at Kyle, three with familiar faces, Simien, Ingris and Zarckro.

"Welcome back son!" said Zarckro proudly "you're looking well!"

Simien ran up to Kyle and hugged him, "I've missed you so much! Oh! And congratulations on your son!"

"Thank you!" laughed Kyle, "It's good to be back here."

Ingris walked forward with the other stranger "Kyle! I have someone here that you'd probably want to meet!"

The stranger who was pretty built in stature with long black wavy hair ran up to Kyle and grasped him tightly and hugged him "What a pleasure to finally meet one of my own kind after so long!"

Ingris continued "That's right! He's one of you! Meet Ratiuch, one of the only full blooded Xornans left in the universe! He's going to fight with us on our side and side by side with you."

"I owe it to one of my only living brothers left! I vow to train you on our way to Alpha Draconis. I will watch over you and teach you the final way of controlling Athunium" said Ratiuch proudly.

"Thank you" replied Kyle "That's so cool!"

"Are you ready?" Ratiuch looked into Kyle's eyes.

"I was born ready!" he replied.

The two of them crashed together in an all-out brawl, sparks flew from every blow. They darted about the ship floor weaving in and out of the onlookers. The strength between the two was unfathomable.

"You're holding back!" Kyle grinned with anticipation.

"So are you!" replied Ratiuch. Darting in for another attack "now we'll step things up a notch!" he opened the palm of his hand and aimed it at Kyle, then a blue ball of energy shot and slammed Kyle into the floor. He stood up and his body was steaming from the heat of the energy that had just crashed into him.

"Oh man! I gotta learn how to do that!"

"You will in time! First you must block and dodge my blasts!" He shot another which again crashed into Kyle.

"Argh! I wasn't ready!" he shouted.

"Neither will you be ready when your enemy pulls that one out of the bag!"

He shoots another and another each crashing into Kyle throwing him to the floor.

"Focus!!" Simien shouted.

"I'm trying!!" he got up and braced himself and was knocked down again by another.

Ingris shouted at Kyle "What are you playing at?! You blocked a blast back on Earth on your first time!"

"Yeah, almost a year ago!" he stood up again and another blast shot at him, this time at the last second, he punched it so hard it disintegrated before everyone's eyes.

"That's more like it" Ratiuch grinned and then shot five more in succession then Kyle screamed out, his body exerted a fierce wind knocking everyone by surprise. Each blast of energy was knocked back, all heading for Ratiuch at full speed. Ratiuch shot out counter blasts which collided with the oncoming ones with epic force that it let out a huge explosion!

Everyone in the ship took cover as smoke submerged the room. Soon enough it settled and all the onlookers watched in awe and then they applauded the amazing performance.

"Excellent, you are ready to control the energy offensively." Ratiuch then sat down. "Come. Sit with me."

Kyle approached and sat on the floor in front of Ratiuch. Kyle watched him hold out his hands in front of him as if he was holding onto an invisible ball, he copied. "It's all about your imagination. You must visualise the energy inside your gut as a blue light. To create the ball you must visualise this energy flowing from your gut up into your chest, then down into your arms and let it leave the palms of your hands and make sure that you imagine it as a solid ball in your hands."

So Kyle began to try and create the energy ball. It wasn't too long until he was able to allow the wispy energy to leave his palms. He just had trouble solidifying it. Ratiuch watched quietly and patiently waiting for Kyle to finally do it. The hours passed and he continued his attempts to create a solid ball.

Simien approached them "There's not much time. We'll be approaching the Hetra Galaxy in the next hour. Prepare yourselves for battle."

Kyle looked at Ratiuch, he looked unsettled.

"You can do it kid. What are you worried about?" laughed Ratiuch "I noticed something about the way you work. When you are backed into a corner you unleash terrifying amounts of power. You got the idea of it now, I'm sure you'll be able to hold your own. Let's take this time to rest before we go into battle!"

It seemed like it was the longest hour of his entire life. The more the minutes passed the more time slowed down, he began to get more and more anxious.

A Lyran soldier by the name of Plashten was gazing through the viewing panel. "There she is. Brace yourselves my friends. We have arrived."

CHAPTER 9
Alpha Draconis

The enormous murky green planet stood idol in the depths of space orbiting around a single red dwarf star. It was so isolated that stars were not even visible in its wake.

The Beamship approached slowly but surely, it came to reach the outskirts of the atmosphere until it disappeared below the clouds.

A low fog covered the surface it was dark and gloomy… there were no buildings or signs of life anywhere. The entire area consisted of murky swamps and dead trees. It was a wasteland.

The ship descended to the ground and touched down on the swamp edge. Ratiuch stepped out followed by Ingris and Kyle.

"Are we even in the right place?" Kyle murmured, slightly distraught.

"This for sure is Alpha Draconis." Ingris replied "This is where we brought them all that time ago."

"No one's here" Ratiuch stated "the planet's an empty shell."

"But that's impossible, where could they all be?"

Ratiuch looked up into the sky, "I sense they are above us."

"They're above us?!" Kyle and Ingris looked up.

"I have a feeling that we're gonna be in for a big surprise."

The three of them looked up into the sky to look for clues but all they could see through the fog was dark clouds covering the sky. It began to rain heavily. Within seconds they were soaked straight through.

"Let's get back to the ship!" Ingris shouted through the rain.

Then out of the clouds thousands of Reptilians began to fall. Each of them landed on their feet with a big thud and surrounded the group, stopping them from going anywhere. They braced themselves for a big fight.

"You dare to show your face here again?!" gurgled one staring straight at Ingris.

"You must be stopped!" Ingris replied "Do you know the cost of your plan?! It's pointless, you could even destroy yourselves!"

Another stepped in and fiercely continued "It's a risk we are willing to take!"

"You've gone mad!"

"The real truth here is, is that you will pay for re-populating our home with vermin!" the third charged at him landing a heavy blow to Ingris knocking him to the ground. The others began to follow, Kyle and Ratiuch stepped in. Soon an all-out brawl took place, energy beams were flying out from all angles. Then, the Beamship door opened. Lyran and Sirian soldiers poured out of the ship screaming their war cries and bombarding the Reptilians with heavy laser gun fire.

The Reptilian who first spoke pulled back, "Retreat!"

The Reptilians began to fly up into the sky at incredible speeds, escaping the battle, there was too much for them to handle.

The surviving soldiers began to cheer and celebrate and their victory, around a quarter of the army had perished in the fight, alongside many Reptilians.

"Whoa, I didn't know they could fly!" Kyle looked up in the sky in awe.

Soon after, Simien stepped out from the ship "It's not over yet."

Silence fell over the army as they all turned to Simien.

"I have discovered the location of their warship."

Plashten, the Lyran soldier from before, stepped out from the crowd "Then we go and finish what we started!"

The crowd began to cheer again, all agreeing with what Plashten said.

Ratiuch interrupted the army and shouted "You all better be ready!" He began to walk between people as if he was briefing them "They've already duplicated their armada to millions! This battle will be to the death, it's all or nothing. We cannot let them achieve their goal!"

The crowd fell silent.

"So, are you cowards ready or what?!"

The crowd began to cheer again as they all began to board the Beamship.

Kyle, Simien, Ingris and Ratiuch began to follow then Kyle stopped. "Hold on a minute. Where's Zarckro?"

Ratiuch turned around and looked through the Reptilian and Lyran remains. The heavy downpour of rain made it hard to see, he walked back out into the rain, and Kyle followed. *Zarckro's not in the ship with the others, I hope he's OK.* Kyle thought to himself. Ingris joined the search.

Then Ratiuch shouted from the distance "Son of a bitch! I found him!"

The Kyle and Ingris ran to him to find Zarckro unresponsive with his face half submerged in a puddle.

Kyle crashed to his knees in the water, looking down on his friend, he couldn't bear seeing Zarckro like this, the rain continued to pour heavily and he thumped his fists viciously into the ground causing water to splash up into his face.

"I can see your tears through the rain, kid" Ratiuch helped Kyle up. "Let's show those animals who the real men are around here."

Kyle nodded, although hurting and full of anger, he followed as Ingris and Ratiuch led him back into the Beamship.

Inside, everyone fell quiet as the three of them boarded; they made way for Kyle and the others. Kyle made his way to the back of the ship, not saying a word. He was dangerously quiet.

Simien walked up to him and asked "Do you want to go now and do what we came here for?"

Kyle continued to look into space with revenge written all over his face and just said one word, "Yes."

CHAPTER 10
The Showdown

The Beamship let off an enormous flash as it crashed with force out of the planet.

Meanwhile, above Alpha Draconis, an incredibly huge warship, twice the size of the planet, moved into place and the Beamship came nose to nose with it.

Then out of the blue, smaller Beamships, thousands of them, just like Simien's old one began to appear behind the big one.

"OK." Simien started "Our armada has arrived and we are ready to battle! I will teleport you all in one by one to different levels of the Reptilian craft, your mission, is to take out any enemy to come across. We cannot let one survive!"

Then groups of soldiers began to disappear in flashes of white light until just Simien, Kyle, Ingris and Ratiuch were the only ones remaining.

"You three are our powerhouses." She said "The others will clear most of the defences up until the path to Blackmist is open. That is where you three come in."

"Then let's take this chance to hone your control skills." Ratiuch led Kyle to a corner of the ship and sat him down on the floor. Kyle continued his training to hold together a ball of energy… he could hear the battle from the other ship raging intensely, he couldn't concentrate.

"I'm really nervous, man" Kyle began to get shaken up.

"Don't be silly kid, you're a powerful warrior! I believe in you!"

Ingris joined them and held his hands apart and he began to create an energy ball, encouraging Kyle and trying to take his mind off of the war.

"C'mon Kyle, you *can* do it!" smiled Simien from a distance.

His confidence started to come back slowly but surely but before he could straighten himself up for another shot they heard a voice in their heads, it was Plashten.

"OK! We're ready for you now! We're on the final floor!"

Then without notice, Kyle didn't even get a chance to stand up, a flash covered them and as the light faded, he found himself inside a dark and gloomy corridor, dark grey metal adorned the walls around him.

"OK, let's go." He said but to his horror, the others weren't with him, he was alone.

Simien spoke to him telepathically, "Kyle! Something went wrong! We've teleported to different sides of the ship, head forward and we'll meet up in the main deck! We've got no time to lose! Get moving!"

Without saying a word, he nodded and began to run through the weaving corridors jumping over dead bodies on the way, soon enough he came across a crossroad in the path. *Which way left or right?*

Strange symbols were written across the walls.

He took the corridor heading left; he came across a doorway and made his way in.

It was a dead end. He turned to make his out and was stopped in his path by a giant Reptilian monster; it screamed a horrific hiss and flew at him at incredible speed, smacking him hard in the face.

Kyle held his balance and then braced himself and the monster threw another blow, heading for Kyle's head. He jumped up and grabbed hold of the monsters arm and pulled it down to the ground ripping it from the shoulder.

The monster fell to its knees screaming again.

Kyle then realised that he was holding onto a severed arm, dripping with blood "Urgh! Shit!" he threw the arm to the ground and shuddered in disgust.

The Reptilian then stood up and looked him in the eye, even though armless, it grinned at him. The fearless creature let out an ear piercing screech, a new arm shot from the open wound in its shoulder - spurting blood up onto a nearby wall.

It charged at him for a third time, he was immobilised in shock from what he had just witnessed, then he hit the floor with an almighty thud.

What now? It can grow its limbs back!

Kyle stood up, thinking of Emily and the baby; he charged at the beast, screaming, smashing into it. He forced it into the gloomy corridors and pushed it into a window causing a crack.

Suddenly a small shard of glass broke off causing a huge pull of suction out into deep, ice cold space.

The strong suction pulled the beast into the small gap in the window. It was trapped, intense suction pulling on its spine. It let out ferocious cries of pain, attempting to fight its way off from the window.

Then a loud crunch filled the room and its face grew wide. Followed by another gut wrenching crunch the suction pulled out its spinal cord and its insides followed. The beast lay dead hanging in the window, the outside of the window surrounding the beast was blood stained.

Kyle stepped back slowly, disoriented from his insane experience. He then snapped out of it as Simien called to him again. "Hurry up Kyle!"

"I'm coming!" he replied.

He ran back down the corridor, heading the right way this time and before he knew it, he came into the main control room of the ship, followed by the other three.

A tall chair was situated at the centre-back of the room in front of the viewing panel which was looking over Alpha Draconis.

A voice spoke from the chair "Welcome, I'm glad you finally showed up!"

The chair spun around to reveal the most terrifying Reptilian of them all. It stood up out of the chair. It was huge compared to all the others that Kyle had seen.

It was purple, it had a long scaly tail that matched its skin, it wore black coloured body armour with a Reptilian symbol on the right of the chest and it adorned a long red cape, Blackmist.

Simien stepped forward "Blackmist, this all ends now."

Blackmist laughed "Just the four of you?!"

Ratiuch stepped forward and stared at Blackmist, confident "We won't even need four to finish you."

He laughed again "Who said it was going to be just me?!" As he said that, he burst an intense amount of energy clearing the area of all obstacles for a fight.

Ratiuch grinned and looked at Simien and Ingris "You guys better get out of here, this could get ugly!" he then looked at Blackmist and laughed "Not that it already is."

Simien looked at Kyle, he nodded with a smile "It's cool, Ratiuch will look after me."

Then with a great flash, Simien and Ingris vanished.

Ratiuch double backed on himself and ran straight at Blackmist, without notice a heavy battle started between the two, Kyle looked on mesmerised at the intense fight that took place before him. These guys didn't cut corners, they got straight to business.

Every blow let off an intense shockwave that ricocheted off every surrounding wall.

But he couldn't just stand there. He had to do something to help, but he couldn't get a hit in edgeways, even if he wanted to. They were going at it way too fast.

The battle continued to rage, no side was backing down, and energy blasts were darting out from the clash and bursting into flames around the ship. Kyle was analysing the way Blackmist fought so he could at least throw in a surprise attack when Blackmist did not expect it. That could throw the fight in Ratiuchs favour.

He came to notice that Blackmist's back was open to an attack so he braced himself and ran for it!

The faster he ran, the more he picked up speed and at the last second he jumped, aiming a kick right to the back of his neck.

Then, in a bizarre turn of events, Blackmist swung around and grabbed hold of Kyle's foot, Ratiuch froze then snapped out of it going in for another hit to let Kyle loose.

It then happened so quickly, but it felt like slow motion.

Blackmist's hand gripped tighter around Kyle's foot, he continued to grip tighter, and Kyle screamed in agony as all the bones in his foot shattered.

Blackmist stared into his eyes and smiled horrifically, still holding onto Kyle's now crushed foot.

Blackmist then swung Kyle across the room, he span on his other foot like a spinning top and once that ankle crushed beneath the pressure, it gave in, his legs parted as he crashed to the floor ripping at the skin and muscles in his groin. He then continued to tumble, breaking bones in his arms and legs until he came crashing into the wall.

He lay there motionless, bleeding from his groin, head and mouth.

Ratiuch's blow finally hit Blackmist, crashing him to the floor and he began to run for Kyle. "Kyle!!"

Then without him realising, Blackmist stood back up and threw an energy wave throwing Ratiuch into the flames that surrounded them.

Blackmist began to walk towards Kyle, who slowly regained consciousness.

Blackmist continued to walk and laughed, "Ha ha! In what reality did you even think that you could put up a fight against me boy?!"

Kyle couldn't move an inch, he couldn't feel his legs.

Blackmist stopped, standing two meters from Kyle; he raised his hand, pointing his open palm at him.

"For eons my home has been calling for my return…"

Thick red wisps of energy began to flow around his hand generating a small red ball which began to grow.

"When I arrive…" He then shouted, firing the massive sphere of red energy "I will be sure to finish your loved ones first!!"

Then suddenly a voice bellowed from the flames, "NOOOOO!!!" Ratiuch jumped from the flames and landed in front of Kyle, facing the deadly blast, protecting him.

Ratiuch threw up his hands as the blast made contact with him, he was pushing at the heavy ball, stopping it from coming any closer, and he couldn't keep it up forever. Soon the blast was going to burn through his flesh, disintegrating him.

Using every ounce of strength to hold it off, he looked back at Kyle, though he was smiling at him, Kyle could see the agony in his eyes.

"You… know…what to do…kid."

The fate of the entire universe was hanging in the balance, despite his broken bones and lack of blood, Kyle pushed up and forced himself onto his broken feet, he couldn't feel the pain thanks to the high amount of adrenaline rushing through him.

"I…believe… in you…" the energy ball slowly ate at him and finally, there was nothing of Ratiuch left. He was gone.

The blast then slowly continued to move towards Kyle.

Kyle had just watched another of his friends die at the hands of the Reptilian monsters, the agony of loss filled his heart. The infuriation in him swelled rapidly.

He was like my brother. He was my best friend. ***YOU KILLED MY BROTHER!! YOU KILLED MY BEST FRIEND!!!!!***

Kyle screamed as an intense fiery blue aura exploded from his body, it soon engulfed him swirling around him like a tornado.

An intense swirling sound filled the room, his hair began to stand on end and shine silver glow and he looked through the approaching energy ball right into Blackmist's eyes. "It ends now."

He let out another deafening roar and to Blackmist's surprise an intense beam of pure blue energy shot from Kyle's glowing body.

The energy shot across the room like a gushing torrent of water, heading straight for the Reptilian king.

"WHAT?!! IMPOSSIBLE!!!" the wave crashed into him with incredible force, it had already disintegrated his limbs, and it pushed him, crushing him into the viewing panel that was looking over the green planet. Within seconds Blackmist was dust.

Then the room fell silent.

The viewing panel began to crack as Kyle's energy field settled, he began to feint.

The ship suddenly lurched forward into the atmosphere of Alpha Draconis, throwing Kyle into the viewing panel. It smashed into thick shards of glass around him, he was then sucked out into the skies of the planet and he began to fall through the clouds.

He was too weak to even try and resist. With the last bit of strength he had, he looked up and the burning warship above him, which was also collapsing into the planet. He was at peace, he smiled. At least he knew that Emily and the child were going to be safe.

Heavy debris fell past him from above, crashing into the ground below; Alpha Draconis began to crack and crumble, throwing up lava meters into the air.

He continued to drop, the wind caressed his numb body, and he then closed his eyes as he fell into the depths of the now exploding planet.

To be continued…

Umar Arar

Athunium

Umar Arar

A Message from the Author:

From the bottom of my heart, thank you very much for purchasing and reading Athunium.

Are you surprised how it just ended? Let's just say that this may not be the only book in the Athunium series!

But I'll let you think about what happened to Kyle, what do you think? Did he perish or did he survive?

I hope you had as much fun reading this story as much as I had writing it. Thank you so much for your support and I'll see you around!

God bless!

Athunium

The Destruction of Alpha Draconis

Debris continued to fall from the burning ship.

The planet crumbled and shook, lava burst up into the air from the newly formed cracks in the ground. The massive falling ship finally crashed into the surface causing a destructive earthquake.

The green murky planet was no longer a green hue; it was now a glowing red hot, crumbling planet, moments away from explosion.

Plumes of hot lava and gas burst through the atmosphere until a devastating explosion cracked the core, splitting the planet into two separate chunks of rock, each then exploded with tremendous force, leaving nothing but dust and rubble floating where the biggest planet in the entire universe once adorned the skies.

Alpha Draconis was no more.

Beyond the devastation a small dark grey triangular shaped craft floated through the floating rubble.

A purple Reptilian wearing the same armour as Blackmist watched over his destroyed home.

"A mere human…"

It clenched its fists tight and let out a blood curdling laugh, "Ha ha ha! Don't you fret father of mine. I will avenge you. Earth will pay the price for its pathetic hero."

With that, the triangular craft turned and slowly headed away from the tattered planet, firing off into space getting further and further until it only resembled a star in the distance.

Alien language translations:

Ayvan – The Language of the Pleiades:

W. – *Nakshi* – The symbol for warrior of Light.

CLHCIT FFSHOUY Q LHDIF – *Galaki insona monaka nakshimina* – The Galactic Federation of Light.

Draconian – The Language of the Reptilians:

N – *En Sthanth* – Symbol for Reptilian royalty.

JVIEV KAF 7107VTU – *Insinith roh mosthin* – Infirmary left, and right Control deck.

Earth

Umar Arar

Alpha Draconis

Athunium

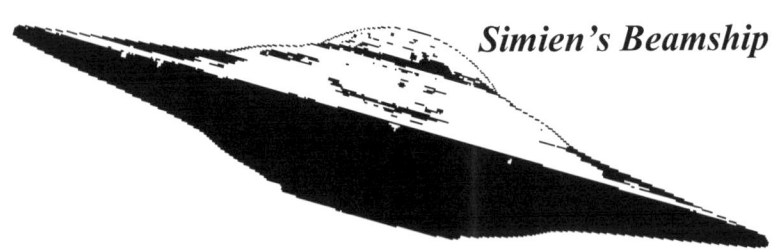

Simien's Beamship

Coming Soon:

Athunium, Part II: A New World Order.